MW01131252

<u>Praise for *The Great Big Ark in the Sky*</u>

"The story is an enchanting tale of acceptance and assurance when a child faces the loss of a pet. The illustrations and placement of the words on the page provide a sense of wonder and adventure suitable for a variety of ages spanning the youngest of listeners to more advanced readers. This book provides an opportunity for families facing difficult times to imagine the possibilities and open the door for processing their loss across faiths."

—Samara Musselman, MT, M.Ed, Early Childhood Educator

"The most significant relationships of a child's life can be those they share with their pets. This book honors these relationships while illustrating the importance of giving kids language to talk about loss and death. I'm thankful that this book continues to expand the options parents have to explore these topics with their children."

—Joy Outland-Brock, LCSW and Therapist

"Reading *The Great Big Ark in the Sky* was a delight. Its tender language and gorgeous child-friendly illustrations pulled me in immediately. What a gentle and kind way to teach children that death is not an end, but a transition. The artistry of Ballard, Hamm, and Koo is on display, and their reverence for the subject of love, loss, and loving again will likely comfort many young and not-so-young alike. Kudos for such a gift."

—Cynthia R. M. Rafala, LPC, LMFT, CCMHC, Counselor and Therapist

"*The Great Big Ark in the Sky* is an absolute must in your child's library! Not only does it tackle difficult subject matter with a gentle word and a sense of wonder, but the illustrations are charming and approachable. A dream of heaven for all of God's creatures has never been so natural or so beautiful."

—Jessica Moretti, MFA, Designer and Illustrator

"People are often young when they first experience the permanence of loss and truly deep sadness that accompanies the death of a beloved animal family member. A cat, dog, guinea pig—it does not matter—the grief is real! I would like to think my Foxhound is sitting next to the helmsman, taking in the sights on *The Great Big Ark in the Sky*."

—H. E. Burchard, DVM, Owner of Amberwood Veterinary Hospital

For Jill and Donald and their beloved dog, Cleopatra: Thank you for inspiring us to write this story and share it with the world. For our faith, family, and friends: Thank you for daring us to imagine.

—Liz and Andrew

ISBN: 978-1-947860-24-7
LCCN: 2018962577

Designed by Michael Hardison
Project managed by Christina Kann

Printed in the United States of America

Published by
Belle Isle Books (an imprint of Brandylane Publishers, Inc.)
5 S. 1st Street
Richmond, Virginia 23219
belleislebooks.com | brandylanepublishers.com

BELLE ISLE BOOKS
www.belleislebooks.com

"We are all creatures of one family."
—St. Francis of Assisi

BY LIZ BALLARD HAMM AND ANDREW BALLARD | ILLUSTRATED BY LUCY KOO

THE GREAT BIG ARK IN THE SKY

BELLE ISLE BOOKS
www.belleislebooks.com

Once upon a day not so long ago, on a hillside not so far away, a little girl turned to her brother and said, "I miss our doggy. I wish he was still here with us."

Looking toward the open sky, the boy replied: "Do you ever wonder where all the animals go when they leave this world?"

Imagine...

There's a special ship that sails through time and space. It travels to many different places along the way, and its voyage is never-ending. It is the Great Big Ark in the Sky.

ALL ABOARD
THE GREAT BIG ARK,
ALL ABOARD!

This hilltop is one of the places the Ark visits.

Here it welcomes aboard any creature,

big or small, who is ready to go on

an epic journey.

Then the Ark sails away

through the clouds,

past the stars,

and beyond the planets.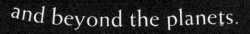

It sails to a beautiful and wondrous place,

a paradise full of the most awesome

love any creature has ever known.

In this boundless place,

the Ark visits many ports of call.

ALL ASHORE
THE DESERT PORT,
ALL ASHORE!

In the desert port, the
roadrunner loves racing
across the sand and feeling
the warm sun
on its back.

In the tropical port, the elephant loves soaking in the cool waters and tasting the sweet fruit from the jungle trees.

ALL ASHORE THE TROPICAL PORT, ALL ASHORE!

15

In the tundra port, the hare loves hopping around and looking out into the endless snowy plain.

In the prairie port, the horse loves galloping freely
in the meadow and smelling the wildflowers.

There are many more ports of call,

too many even to count.

But on each voyage, the Ark always sails to
one place where the love shines forever.

This is the city port...

...and in the city port, the dog loves seeing his old friends and hearing the joyful music play.

ALL ASHORE
THE CITY PORT,
ALL ASHORE!

"You see," said the boy to his sister,

"the Great Big Ark in the *Sky* is forever sailing...

"...bringing all of God's creatures home."

THANK YOU to our family, friends, and furry pals, both here and beyond, who have encouraged and inspired us on this long and winding journey.

Thank you to our parents, Pat and Bill Ballard, who have always been our biggest champions through every dream we've ever pursued. Much love to you both from Monkey and Bunny Ribbit. Yes, reader, that's right, it's Ribbit.

To our brother, Taylor, thank you for inspiring us with your own amazing talent and great capacity for kindness. To our beautiful new sister, Hailey, thank you for joining our crazy tribe and bringing fun and laughter along with you.

To Liz's husband and the love of her life, Andrew Hamm, you have been our rock of support as we've climbed this mountain. Thank you for being an incredible husband, father, and artist. To Ruby and Gabriel, and any children still in the stars, you are the greatest joys in life.

Thank you to our publisher, Robert Pruett of Belle Isle Books, for believing in our story and making our dream come true! Thank you to Christina, Michael, and Belle Isle's terrific team for helping to put this book together and get it out into the universe.

And a special thanks to our friend and the most epic illustrator-warrior ever, Lucy Koo, who took everything that was in our minds and transformed it into beautiful art.

—Liz and Andrew

LIZ BALLARD HAMM & ANDREW BALLARD are siblings who grew up in rural Virginia, where they spent their childhood exploring the foothills of the Blue Ridge with their dogs. Liz, Andrew, and their younger brother, Taylor, all shared a passion for storytelling from an early age. Liz and Andrew both went on to study theatre — Liz at Catawba College and Andrew at James Madison University. Their professional paths first crossed shortly after college; they both went to work for Virginia Repertory Theatre, where they performed children's theatre together for young audiences across the country.

Today, Liz enjoys exploring the wilds of Richmond, VA with her husband, Andrew Hamm, their children, Ruby and Gabriel, and their loving dog, Boba. Liz is a student at Bon Secours Memorial College of Nursing. Andrew is currently engaged in postgraduate studies at the University of Virginia. He now adventures through life as an actor, writer, and teacher living in Culpeper, VA, with his dog, Luke, at his side. Between Liz and Andrew, they also have six cats who keep it real: Rosalind, Henry, Hermione, Luna, Fleur, and Binx.

The Great Big Ark in the Sky is Liz and Andrew's first picture book. More information about the authors and their book can be found at their website, greatbigark.com

LUCY KOO is a South Korean-born artist who creates detailed illustrations inspired by her childhood living in Seoul, where her home had a view of Bukhansan Mountain. After moving to the States, she attended Virginia Commonwealth University, studying communication arts and developing her skills as an illustrator. Today, Lucy pursues her passions in art and design as a suburbanite living outside Washington, D.C. Her portfolio can be found on her website, lucykoo.com

CPSIA information can be obtained
at www.ICGtesting.com
Printed in the USA
BVHW022326220219
540891BV00003B/7/P